Last Breath in Sutherland

D1759991

A Collection of Scottish Short Stories

By David Tallach

For Kevin with best wishes,

David Tallach

Copyright

First Printing:
ISBN 978-1-326-23706-6
East Highland Gothic Press
87 Alltan Place
Inverness, IV2 7TA

For Becca

Table of Contents

Table Of Contents (continued)

Collaborators

I was unsure if I could trust our new friend. Her eyes glittered coldly across the campfire. My Lancaster was gone, with half my crew. Just Bob and I were left, shot down in a strange land where we could barely speak the language. I knew a little French, had been meaning to build it up given the ops we were running… but always too tired. Our contact in the French Resistance had failed to turn up. Bob and I were shocked, tired and hungry, our uniforms tattered, little proof against the cold. We had buried our parachutes. We were about to leave the prearranged spot, a barn on the edge of Poitiers, when a woman came out of the dark. She beckoned to us. Bob pulled his gun, but she laughed and beckoned again. We followed her inside. She had a fire burning, cooking a pot over it. There was the smell of something that could have been rabbit. 'English pilots,' she said, nodding and smiling.

'Scottish, actually,' I said, but she took no notice. We helped ourselves to the stew, with some plates she provided. 'Is the farm yours?' I said, pointing at the buildings. She did not seem to understand.

'Rest here,' she said. She pointed at the straw. Bob settled down for the night. I wasn't too sure about the straw, being allergic to grass and its derivatives, but it was better than being outside in November.

I woke to a screech that had me reaching for my gun. A shadow flew across the rafters, but it was only an owl. I should have realised. I had been brought up on a farm, in the Mearns, north of Dundee. I settled back to sleep. I woke again, in the early morning, my gun still close to me. I could hear voices, out in the courtyard. I wriggled through the straw to get a better view. There was the sound of a motorbike, revving into life. I saw several Nazis in uniform, searching the courtyard and fanning out. Some had dogs. I wriggled back inside the barn to try and find Bob. 'We have to get out!' I hissed, in case he was still asleep. There seemed little prospect of escape. I found my way to the side of the barn, and drew my revolver.

Part of the wall came down in front of me, on an unseen mechanism. I started to wonder if the farm itself was real. Blinking in the sunlight, I could hear the dogs being restrained. I flung my weapon down, still finding it difficult to see. A woman stepped forward in front of the uniformed men, and picked up my revolver. She smiled, and for a moment I could not recognise the woman from last night. She seemed so much younger. 'Jam, jute and journalism,' she said, in a perfect English accent. 'Isn't that right, Dundee boy?'

State Of Independence

David MacLeod tossed aside his tricornered hat as he walked into the bar. 'Good afternoon, Mrs Fox,' he said to the landlady. She nodded back, clearing glasses from the tables. The blackboard behind the bar read 'Steak pie 1/6' in red, blue and white chalk. He crossed over to a table, and sat down next to an older man, his face very lined. 'Hallo, Rex,' he said. Rex smiled and finished his draught. David nodded to Mrs Fox for more drinks. 'Cloudy day,' said Rex slowly, looking out the window with rheumy eyes at the landscape.

'Yes,' said David. 'Many more clouds are coming.' Rex coughed.

'Reckon there might be about… forty south-west.' He fell to coughing as Mrs Fox provided the drinks. David smiled at her.

'Many customers today?'

'It's as you see it.' Her voice was flat and toneless. He paid her and she left them.

'I last saw the sun sinking to the west,' said David.

'That is where it usually goes,' said Rex patiently. 'But today, I saw it rise forty in strength.' David looked over Rex's shoulder. He could have been mistaken, but the menu now read, 'Fish pie 3/4.' He thought nothing of it. He drank deeply of the wine. It reminded him of his former campaign against the French, some twenty years ago. There came a gust of wind as the door opened to admit two men in long travelling cloaks. They looked intently at the menu, still clearly outlined in red, white and blue chalk.

Mrs Fox's tone was markedly more friendly to them. 'You'll be having the special,' she said. The visitors turned and raised their hats to David and Rex. David nodded briefly, considering the information Rex had given him. This was a different front to the one he was used to fighting on.

'Forty,' he mused aloud. 'Forty... like a fort.' It seemed unaccountably funny. Rex slumped headfirst onto the table. David found his reactions slowing, vision blurred. He looked up at the menu. If he had been able to make out the words, he would have read, 'Pheasant 2/3' in red, white and blue chalk. The two men who had come in after him moved silently to stand behind him, casting a shadow like the gallows. There was the sound of a musket being cocked. He heard Mrs Fox's voice behind him.

'This is for my husband. You may remember him, *Colonel*. You had him shot.'

Big Yellow Taxi

'The Council voted for *what?*' asked Joni sharply, coming home and draping her school tie over a chair. It was May, and it was raining. Summer seemed to attract rain in Aberdeen, if anything.

'We lost,' said Dylan glumly. 'They're going to gut the Gardens.' Joni's lips twitched slightly at the alliteration, then she frowned.

'You might think that two-hundred-year-old trees had some kind of a voice... heritage and all.'

'As for a philanthropist- what is one, really?' said Dylan, hands in pockets, staring out at the rain. 'Someone who builds hospitals, perhaps. Not someone who destroys a city centre park just to put up more wretched shops and a *car park*.'

'Talk about a mind of metal,' said Joni, her day's attempt at Higher Biology almost forgotten. 'They should have gone for that theatre to one side of it, if they had to develop it at all. How many people really want this... development, anyway? Do they really think ruining the centre of town will work, when shops are dying on Union Street, just a stone's throw away?'

'Ah, it's all about greed,' said Dylan dismally, watching the rain pour down the windows with an air of detachment. 'Money, money, money.'

Recovery Position

I don't want to let her go. The machine keeps her alive… just. The odd flicker I see in her face, and no-one else does. There is that necklace, with the dolphins, the one I gave her for her birthday. It moves with her breathing, the inhuman hiss and click of the machine behind her a ghastly thing we would rather do without. We will not need it for long.

I feel a nurse touch my arm. They want me to make a decision. Keep her here, in the land of the living, or let her go, like some blessed balloon. First the nurse, then the doctor, are firm about this. They want more. They want her to benefit others. I want her to be there for me. Hiss, click. Hiss, click. There is a kind of eloquence to it in ventilating her life, propping her up, but it is nothing compared to her poetry, her life, her voice. I so want to hear it again.

They say our time is up. They need the bed, apparently. What do they think she is doing, lying here for her own convenience? A thousand times, I would rather have her in our bed. They say her condition will not change, no matter what. I like to think of her sailing away with the dolphins, away up the loch, strong and powerful. The lights are going out. I cannot bear to look.

Hunter, Gatherer

The man whose skull had a certain impact, and now resides in the British Natural History Museum, known as the Cheddar Man, once strode the wild woods of Palaeolithic Britain, spear in his hand. He was dressed in deerskins, and sought more of them, perhaps from the same herd. He walked in a regular, loping stride, his ears attuned to the faintest rustle among the autumn leaves . He was known in his tribe as a great hunter, one who provided for his very extended family.

He had been walking for a long time, most of that day. He paused to eat some of the nuts and berries in a pouch he carried at his belt. Sometimes, he thought he detected a movement behind him, but concentrated on the herd in front. There would be plenty of meat and skins, even from one. He judged the wind, waited for the right moment, and hurled his spear. It pinned the beast through the neck. He moved swiftly over to kill it. The dying red rays of the sun painted him in a gory costume as he went about the process. His spear lay by his side. He turned to look for it, then realised it had gone. He stood up by the stones, now casting evening shadows. There was a movement on the other side of the circle, then he stood transfixed, as the stag had been. 'You!' spat a female voice he knew well. 'You and that other woman!'

Bone Of My Bone

'She's facing due east,' I said, wiping my hands of the familiar dust as I stood up in the trench. Dee shrugged, still further down in the trench.

'We know she was buried with things they valued. Or things they thought she should value.'

'Are you thinking... late Iron Age?'

'Maybe. Pass me the trowel.' We worked in the shadow of a neighbouring broch, a tall dark tower from the period just named. We had a grant from the Council to probe the mystery of these remains in the Orkney Islands for a short time, as always. We were on Shapinsay, near the shore. So many crumbling remains, washing away into the sea; limited time, money, expertise to examine them all. We liked to think we could provide the third part, anyway, if there was rarely enough of the first two.

***

'Neil! Neil!' I woke up from my tent, and wandered outside. I thought I heard a voice. There was nothing but the cold, exposed remains of the past; a banquet of bones, in the long barrow, the trench. The light rain washed at me as I shivered, still half asleep, and jammed my hands in my pockets. I remembered our last dig. I remembered it so well. I wished she were still with me, indeed, not buried four thousand miles away in her native land.

What was I doing here, excavating the past again?

Axe

I'm a cut above, you know. I may have left my silk robe at the Palace, but my dignity is intact. I prayed this morning, for the last time. I tried to make them see sense about the churches, but they would not have it. So now, they will not have me. It is cold, but I think they feel it more than I do. My breath comes out visibly. It almost reminds me of my favourite charger, the time van Dyck painted me. Happy days.

Ah, there is the scaffold. The steps point to a throne higher than these… peasants can ever imagine. I walk slowly, to my new coronation. Every step seems to echo in the sharp, clear air. Do they repent, now, of what they did to me, for putting me on trial, for the loss of so many lives in the wars? Here is my praying stool, from which I may never rise as I am now. It has the aspect of an anvil, for readying for battle, forging weapons. I have mettle enough.

The man in the black hood stands to the side. Yet he is merely an instrument of God's will. He may not kill me, be it but God's will. I undo the long scarf around my neck, keeping a level gaze. I dare him to turn away. Then I kneel to my altar, as a swallow dives, immaculate, already at peace. Come on. Chop, chop.

We Hold These Truths

'We don't tend to have gargoyles in Scotland,' I said. 'The theology's different.'

Dee was just getting out of her side of the car. She squinted up at the eaves of the church.

'Sure, no stone monsters there,' she said. 'Kinda disappointing.' The church near

Beauly was isolated, clearly visible from half a mile down the road. I pointed up to the lintel.

'Look. An interesting year for your country.'

'1776. Oh, sure.'

'You have to admit, it is a pity about all that tea.'

'When are you going to let that go? No taxation without representation. Now, are

we going in? Oh look, a lizard.' A large hollow metal lizard adorned one side of the former

church, now an art gallery. She studied it, head to one side. 'We certainly have a large variety

of reptiles in Florida.'

'Don't I know it! I remember the snake episode. How you put that wee thing

outside.'

'I am not cursed with a fear of snakes. I established it was harmless... probably a

baby.' She preceded me through the door of the gallery, lowering the hood of her jacket. We

were alone apart from the attendant, struggling downstairs from the gallery with an artefact of

some kind.

'I'm afraid the land of your ancestors is like this... pretty much all year round,' I

said. She signed her name in the visitors' book, propped up on the broad sill of one of the

diamond-paned windows. She gazed out at the graveyard beyond, rising up a steep hill.

'Beauly is the seat of the Highland, or 'Lovat' Frasers,' I said. 'History's usually

written by the winners... the same reason you get MacKays in Sutherland. Robert the Bruce gave lands to the chiefs who'd supported him at Bannockburn.' She did not reply.

Dee moved over to one of Allan MacDonald's landscapes.

'Intense,' was all she said.

'I think you get a better perspective if you stand back,' I said, surveying the winter scene from the other side of the one large room. The pews were long gone. I tried not to think of where a couple would have stood to get married. The rain pattered on the roof. Dee pointed to the lizard, just visible from one window, and smiled.

'Who says ya don't have gargoyles?'

Bubble And Squeak

'How much is it worth again, Pa?'

'Ten cents, and no more. That's enough for you.'

'Is it enough for you as well?'

'Never mind your cheek.' Tommy held up a rat by the tail. It squirmed and squeaked. He took a rock to it, and it stopped squeaking. 'Throw it in the bucket,' directed his father. A hurricane lamp threw a fitful light over their faces. Tommy's father held it up, and shadows fled before it. The damaged sewers of San Francisco rose up around them, a captive city released, the lost hanging gardens of Babylon into the open air. There was the pollution of the stench, broken pipes, fallen snakes, endless snakes, their heads crushed yet still roaming free. And their servants, the rats. Tommy held another, smaller lamp. He swung it to and fro. The shadows waltzed. 'Don't do that,' said his father sharply. 'You don't want it to go out.'

'Aw, Pa! D'you reckon we'll see the Suns take on the Mudcats again, like we did last week?'

'That was before the earthquake,' said his father grimly, leading the way. 'The baseball field's been used for the casualties since then.'

Tommy's ears were alert for another squeak. 'Must be a family of them over here, Pa. The big mammies are worth more, eh?'

'Fifty cents, son.'

'That's get me a… season ticket, sweets, ciggies?'

'Don't let me hear you've taken that up, at your age. Worth another beating.'

'Bruce and the other kids do. Behind the-'

'I don't want to hear it.' Tommy set his lamp down. The darkness rippled and squeaked. He struck fast with a wooden stick, behind the pipe. 'Mind your fingers, son. You don't want to get bitten by those brutes.' There was one final squeak. Tommy picked up his bucket again.

'And if I killed plenty mammy-rats, I'd get dollars…'

'Us or them, son. You know why we're here.'

'Sure. Defending our family. Protectin' the neighbourhood.'

'That's right. Plenty people died in that earthquake, without this… as well.'

'Why do people die like that, Pa? The coughing, the boils, the swellin' like cabbages?'

'Plague, son. Maybe like a visitation from God. This city has its sins, you know. Things no-one ever sees, but God knows about. Sometimes he has to punish them for it. Like you and the bicycle last year.'

'Oh. Like that, eh?'

'Yeah. Just like that. So be warned.'

'Sure will.' Tommy lagged behind for a moment, swinging his lamp more vigorously. His father turned a corner. Tommy tripped, and broke his lamp. 'Pa? Where are you?' There was an echo, a rustle, and a squeak.

The Kingdom Of Heaven

'Hear us, O Lord. Have mercy.' The words in Latin echoed around the clearing. Brother Andrew looked over at the freshly-dug mound of earth. All around it were recent crosses, in this part of the wood, bordering the village. The mound before him was still raw, the soil turned only that morning, a light brown almost like dried blood. His voice rose and fell, in the cadences he had recently learned in the monastery. Established as a closed order, some of the brothers were now released into more public service, owing to the dire need for offices at funerals. He fell back naturally to what he knew best.

'God's wrath is among us,' he announced confidently, then paused as he thought of the local priests who had also died, necessitating his own presence here. The family of the deceased stood before him, looking from him to the new grave. 'But also God's sorrow… the comfort of our Lord is very near,' he finished.

The father stood, hands callused in his farm labour, his heavy-set face blank. The mother stood by him, clutching their latest baby. It was coughing and squirming into her shawl. A girl of about six fidgeted by them, looking over at the grave. She seemed suspicious of Brother Andrew.

He was thinking of the cloistered silence he was used to, and how while there he would gain from keeping silent, rather than like this. Anything but this. He had to do something. There was no garden to tend here, other than the graves daily increasing around him. There were still prayers to be said, but so few to take comfort from them. He had to do something.

He took a deep breath, and motioned to the gravedigger to start filling in the hole. Then Brother Andrew reached over and picked up a twig, recently fallen from a beech in autumn. He cleared his throat, awkwardly.

'I… will remember you. Our Lord will hear, and answer. I am his messenger, and he will hear you, day and night. I will… continue to say offices for you.' He swiped his back with it, once, twice. He set his face to the open road, beyond the clearing, out of the wood. He had to do something. There was the regular sound of the earth being shovelled back into the grave. The baby coughed, and squirmed.

Kite

'It's time to think of something else,' I said, putting the finishing touches to the wooden crossbeam, and measuring the bright red paper on top. 'It's time to do *new* things.'

'Easier said than done, sometimes.'

'Oh, I know. I've been meaning to do this for a while.' I showed Robert what I had been doing, the crossbeam now with the red paper stretched over it, and he helped me to fasten it down.

'There. Almost ready to fly… how long has it been now?'

'Three months.' I paused with the kite under my arm before leaving the room. 'Three months since she left me. She had her… reasons.' He followed me outside. The house was a simple croft, once derelict, now half-restored. We had come out there on a Saturday to do some work on it. It wasn't fully habitable yet. It was in a lonely place, lonely made bright by the blue sky and the company, my cousin and old friend.

The wind tore at my unfastened jacket, almost threatening to whip it away. We stood on a rock a little way from the croft. I held it at arm's length, stared at it for a moment. It was like a face with no features. Its tail hung down like a pigtail. I felt like blushing for a moment.

'Are you ready to let go?' Robert shouted over the wind, almost in my ear. 'Are you ready?'

Charnel-House

'We live, and learn.' Haddon stood at the foot of a corpse, his breath rasping through the long, beak-like mask. He almost gagged on the sweet herbs at the end of it. Berwick inclined his head. He was similarly dressed, like a walking bird of prey. It was late in the Edinburgh morgue.

'We live, when so many do not.'

'We are in the hands of God,' said Haddon.

'Perhaps too easy an answer.' Haddon coughed again. Berwick looked up sharply, his beak-mask jerking with it. 'Are you all right?'

'Oh, yes, yes.' Haddon coughed, and inhaled more of the herbs than he had meant to. He clutched the side of the rail by the coffin.

Berwick consulted his notes. 'This patient died... of a contraction of the humours... in his bed.'

Haddon laughed, and started to cough again. Berwick looked sharply at him, the impassive mask dull in the pallid half-light. 'Anyone can see that.'

Berwick made some notes in his records. 'All in order.' His breath rasped through the mask.

Haddon's breath came more quickly. He resembled a bird, trailing a broken wing. 'All the world... all... a great cathedral... glory, the lights...'

Berwick ceased writing, his quill scratching the darkness with a predatory edge. He examined his records, again. So many names, struck through as they died. 'Of course,' said Berwick severely, 'you mean the local kirk. None of that high church… officiary.'

Only two candles burned in the desolate, cold stone room. One at the head of the corpse, the other by the writing-desk. The light flickered over the silent head, throwing the plague symptoms into relief. Berwick peered again at the grotesque swollen neck, with its burst black cluster like a rotten fruit.

'That's one he won't be taking to market…' he muttered. 'What think you?' There was a heavy silence. Berwick turned around. His colleague lay fallen, his mask to one side, the herbs spilling out. He approached the body carefully, maintaining his detachment. He laid the mask to one side, and carefully examined Haddon's body. The neck was clean. He detected a cross on a chain beneath his vestments, and frowned. Berwick sighed, laid out Haddon's body, and sat beside him, inspecting him in the fitful light. Across the street, in the early morning, came the first cry.

'Bring out your dead!'

A Twist In Her Sobriety

It's all about mood. The colour of her eyes, the sound of her voice, her folded arms, the shadow of the old railway viaduct... that mood, on a clear autumn day. A grand piano, the deep mahogany tone of it. She stands with her arms folded under the viaduct, waiting for a train that never comes. The grass has grown, literally, over the track. She moves to look up the road, hand on one hip, waiting. A gypsy caravan has long gone, the boat has sailed. Maybe, just maybe, it's going to rain. There is that smell in the air: the anticipation of autumn, the living, breathing and dying that goes on all at once... fungus laying claim to the trees, kind of relishing the dying heat of summer and the waking frost of winter. It is at once the rotting hand of summer and the rising hand of winter. Those railway tracks above are *old*, faded, corrupted... no-one ever stops here any more. So what is she waiting here for? She seems immune to the world at large, looking at the sky, going with the mood. She turns, looks right at you, challenging, an unspoken question: *Are you coming with me?*

(Police want to know the whereabouts of this woman. She was last seen by this viaduct, on the 6th October, 1988.)

Ask For Me Tomorrow

March

Rain spilling down on the edge makes a mockery of my work. This is the open space I chose, a green rectangle opened up, the standard size. I was mowing it just last summer, like the rest of the grounds. Lifting the turf in rhythm now, slap, scraping the surface of the ground, a raw wound opened, the top black as dried blood. Work regularly, cutting through the layers. The first daffodils are out, I pause, look at them briefly, resting a hand on my spade. Examine my calluses, smile at my collection. Rain falls persistently, a month to Easter. The sky cloudy, cumulo-nimbus. Working regularly, a trench of sorts. Like my grandfather in the First World War, his kilt, the lice, rats, duckboards by Verdun. Sinking down, the sticky earth casts shadows, freshly cut, moist loam. Discipline. My working clothes originally dark blue, stained with earth. I am getting hot, going down like a manmade elevator, finger pressed on the button to the basement. Below, the root of all things. And Australia. The space is not required until tomorrow. I like the quiet, time to myself. The space is rising around me, a brown box to contain another. Boxed in. Another pause, looking out at the sky above. The church spire is the only landmark from here. Then my relief comes, time to get out. It's not as if I am six feet tall. And so I rise, rise to my lunch, my part over.

June

Sweat. The roses in full bloom: I squirt them for greenfly. Walking around the grounds. Shirt sleeves. The grass grows quickly, I return often to trim the borders encroaching on each other, plants vying with each other to run the place. Last burial in late May, a spot beneath a cherry blossom tree. Sun is warm. From a distance comes the slow bustle of the town, a steady grumble I can afford to ignore here. The River Ness runs fast, cold and deep. River of water of life. Passing me by. Flowers and wreaths on some graves. In my handiwork, I disturbed the earth, opened a door, closed by the minister and then sealed by me. River goes ever on. Slow, hazy day, unusually hot. People lie out on the green banks across the river. Perhaps they are waiting to cross. Maybe they need a ferryman to take them over, maybe I am he. Flowers full of life: bees, pollen, humming. Keep the grounds tidy. Bend to pick up occasional litter. Lunch: cheese and pickle sandwiches. Back to trimming, get the mower started. Begin at one side, continue, circling older gravestones, some sunk and leaning, subsidence. Other heads are leaning, further down. Cutting the long spears of grass, reaching up as if to tickle the sombre grey stones into life. The Day of Judgement. All the chaff shall burn. The grass is ordered now, shortened. Days like grass. The cherry blossom falls. Full bloom.

September

The leaves keep falling, onto my shoulders, down into the new rectangle I am cutting into the earth. Red, yellow, brown, brown as the earth baked from a long hot summer. Heavy work. Patterns of life, patterns of death. Hearing a baby's cry, looking up, my hair tousled, filthy, earth on my working clothes. The mother soothes the child, rocks the pram. The river is clear today, sparkling. I return to my haven, cutting the familiar trench, wounding the soil to close over the head of another, keep them shut forever and a day. An apple fallen from a tree, its boughs outstretched near me, an invitation. The wind blows in a gust, the leaves rustle, the green apple rolls over and over. Suddenly I do not like it, it rolls towards me, round and shiny and ominous as a green skull, blank and baleful. It rolls to the edge of my fearful pit, and stops. I knock it with my spade, send it tumbling back. The earth is dry and crumbly, seeming ripe for this particular harvest. Shift and cut. Time for my break, rise from the row now three feet deep, saunter over to a bench for my lunch, corned beef sandwiches. The slight wind is pleasant with the sun, trees rustling. I close my eyes and rest for a moment. Something nudges my foot. An apple returns. Then they all start to fall.

December

Cold, crisp darkness. The ground is hard, indifferent to sorrow or regret. Frost diamonds sparkling, the whole surface engaged to death, cold and beautiful. I sit on the bench again, late afternoon, sun setting over the river, shining off the pedestrian suspension bridge. The ground has gone to sleep, locked off for the winter, but I ensure it is tidy, free of litter, sweets, mince pie packets. The trees seem dead, conifers silent as Quakers. There are evergreens over by the church, thick and green. No snow, but a hard frost. Sparkles. A child falls and cries, cutting herself on the hardness. Her mother picks her up and takes her away to a world of warm blankets and hot drinks. School is finished today, children leaving for the holidays. Here it is cold, cold. If the ground needs to be opened, it will take a digger. My arms are getting stiff. Mechanical remembrance. Turn of the soil, seedtime and harvest, turnover, regular clockwork, machines rolling on, tick tock. I stand up, feet crunching on the frozen grass. Some apples from the autumn are still there. I walk between the stones, thinking of this lost city of friends. I had the last care of them. This is my own plot in the corner, this is my place, here I'll stay, for I do like it well. Ask for me tomorrow.

The News From Moidart

'The news fae Moidart come yestreen

Will soon gar mony ferly,

For ships o'war have just come in

And landed Royal Charlie.'

The sun lit up the country around Glenfinnan in August with gold that vanishes,

like an ill-fated wedding. A waiting party stood at the harbour, full of all the expectation of a

new marriage, one to join a country with her ruler, one who, they thought, should never have

been away. As the Young Pretender disembarked, a great banner was raised, one that flew a

rose-like symbol, the white cockade.

He had had pain for some time. Coughing last Christmas, hanging up a picture of

the west coast, the spare nails sticking out from his mouth. The sensation came and went like

needles in his chest. He gritted his teeth and made more jokes. His duties involved seeing

people, talking with them of their problems. They noticed his pallor in the New Year.

Footsteps from the past. Jostling, marching on the road south, walking with

purpose. Some pressed into service, threatened with burning from their homes. Down to the

borders for their first clash, taking the largely unmanned garrisons by surprise.

He should have been in the record books. Surviving a transplant at a time when

transplants were in their infancy, suffering many nights of pain, much of the fighting done in his mind. The will to hang on flowed out from his mind to his faltering body. He had had worse before than these present troubles.

They advanced through the autumn, the government's garrisons short of men, focussed on an attack south of their shores. They had no thought of danger from the north, thinking those wild lands tamed with roads and new bureaucracy from the last rebellion. Even the King became afraid, following his soldiers across the Channel.

The coughing continued, the irritation behind it spreading in silence. Early summer came to his world, the trees in Caithness branching out. He visited a glass factory, saw the calm of the beach outside. The everlasting tide ground the rocks into sand, the sand to become glass. Distorted as it was blown, changed into its next life. Through a glass, darkly. There was an hourglass on his work desk at home. He thought of his past travels. The Egyptian sword, the complete *Encyclopaedia Americana*, the painting of the placid Native American in a canoe on equally still waters. How many books he had. He cut short a walk he had planned, feeling the pain. Living alone. However lively his manner with others, there was always the return to the stillness, the dark at night.

Then came Black Friday in December, the one vote that won the outcome for retreat. At Derby, within 200 miles of their object of London, amid much squabbling they abandoned their goal and began to return north.

At last he had to admit something was wrong. He had seen quite a few doctors in his time, had lived longer than some predicting his death. He passed the time of day with the local people in the waiting room. Samples taken, results awaited. Work continued, it had long been a solace to him. He studied and wrote and prepared to speak. The ship of his body had been in storms before. The phlegm in his throat turned bloody.

Such a dispirited army. What was the point in rising, only to disperse in such a manner? Already defeated by their own side. What had been done could not be undone: battles could not be unfought, the dead raised.

The test results came back as soundings from the depths. Reason could not fathom it, too dark, beyond knowing. He went back to his glass. A third-generation mineral. He looked out at the bay through the rain drizzling at the window. He would pack to go to hospital in Inverness. He had sampled hospitals from London to Winnipeg. He felt grim but resolute, looking around the best room in his modest house. The end of his work loomed, and much of his identity with it. A large picture of colourful, swaying trees was the most striking feature in the room. Another country, in his youth.

The army marched over the border, short on provisions, growing steadily more tired and less disciplined. The nature of their retreat dimmed already low expectations. The recalled army of the establishment pursued them from the south.

He made arrangements about his house, went down to the old Highland capital by train. He had relatives there. He felt oppressed, as though the world were sinking. The hospital was warm. All around him, suffering people with their own stories. He was still keenly interested in others. He attended his niece's wedding, returned exhausted. A strange kind of banqueting hall, but his it was.

The rebels retreated, sometimes through roads built since the last rebellion. The romance of a golden August was long past. The final battle loomed, and even there they would not hold the high ground.

His friends and relations came and went. One by one, torches guttering and fading. As autumn became winter, he moved into the hospice. Life grew colder and slower.

Often in a dark tunnel now, he thought of the past. His people awoke on a raw April morning, on a field near Inverness. On the march from Nairn the night before, they had had nothing to eat. The sleet came down as the government army stood waiting, better fed, better armed. He rose with his family and faced the fate before them. At the other end of the field lurked fear itself, black cockades as coals, red coats as firebrands. Like surgery, the clash was coming, and their knives were hungry.

Muckle Flugga

Joiner turned his bruised face to the light. 'We must get it going,' he shouted above the storm. Henderson scowled, his face grey in the fading daylight. 'We can sort this later,' Joiner insisted, pushing open the door to the lighthouse and pointing the way up the stairs. Henderson paused, but not for long. Joiner paused to collect some more oil from the crew room during their ascent, their shadows going before them on the stairs like puppets. Joiner reached the lamp room first, and fished in his pockets for matches. Henderson stood behind him at the head of the stairs, arms folded, not quite entering. 'You know what to do,' said Joiner without turning round.

Henderson sighed and approached the great beacon, huge and dark in the declining day, almost like an elephant in the room. 'My brother is a gentleman,' he said stiffly, 'like any true man who serves at sea.' Joiner let out a bark of a laugh. Henderson bunched his fists, ready to strike him again.

'Later,' said Joiner with a nod out to sea. 'We must get it going. We must, for the sake of all those men sailing and serving in the Crimea, gentlemen or not.' Henderson checked the light, and nodded. Joiner struck a match and held it up to the great eye, which flickered like a waking iris and winked into life. They stood in silence, watching the sea grow dark around them. The watching was also a lifeline, in their work.

'My brother,' said Henderson, 'is a hero who will stand up to any man alive. As he's not here to stand up to you, I had to do that duty for him.' Joiner lit his pipe, the orange glow now the only clear indication where he stood in the intervals when the light flashed away from him.

'My father died,' said Joiner, 'in the wars with Napoleon. He told me enough about a sailor's life. It's one any wise man would avoid. But still, our light is here, and we have to serve them.' His pipe emitted a strong-smelling smoke. Henderson advanced on him. The light flashed around him so that Joiner was dazzled. He felt Henderson's grimy hands around his throat as they backed towards the guard rail, leading out onto a platform. Joiner's pipe fell and broke.

'I want you to stop my brother from dying!' said Henderson, growing frantic. 'Can you? I want you to stop it!'

We Two Are Coffins

My loved one went ahead of me, in the plague. I could not stop loving him, even though he grew black boils and sweated and called for his mother, long dead. I nursed him all I could, with the sweet water and the herbs and singing hymns softly. There was no other comfort. Here in Crail, east Fife, so many are taken in the storms. Death has a banquet in the rough weather, licking his lips with the huge waves that come and strike the houses on the seafront. We live two streets away from the harbour, glad to survive on a trade that does not depend so much on the weather, and its wickedness. It's not just coffins he builds, of course; he works with the architects and the learned people, they make use of him. I am sure his work has been the means of bringing comfort to many when this outbreak started. Death walks the cobbles outside: we hear him coming with the squeak of the barrow morning and night, coming to pile up the dead for burial. That is an affront, in a way: an affront to my husband's trade, to his way of being. He would never have stood for it. Those people should be buried properly. I like to think we can go with more dignity than drunks taken home from the tavern. My husband's last work stands here in the parlour, the good room facing the street. I wanted something better for him, so I put him in it. It was quite a struggle. I read the Bible over him, and nailed down the lid. It was meant for someone else, but he never came for it. I do not think he ever will, now. There is the question of where my husband should be buried. It is not a very pressing question to me. I felt the boils grow under my arms when I sweated to shove him into a decent resting place, like the child we will never have. I roll my sleeves up and watch them, calmly. Oh they are ugly, like mould, but they will bring me to him soon and for that I bless them. The wind howls outside. I cough more often. I hold a napkin to my mouth, see the blood on it and smile. Again, I hear the barrow outside. Squeak, squeak.

A Black Bridleless Horse

'Can't you *feel* it?' said Caz, shivering as she turned her back on the railway track. It was a railway track no longer in fact, but a cold desolate path, stretching out across half the length of the Black Isle. If I tell the truth, I was not sorry to see her shiver, for it gave me a chance to comfort her. I reached out and held her hand. She was wearing gloves. 'I hope no-one perishes on this old road tonight,' she said, dark eyes flicking back over the long earthen track.

'Why should they?' I asked softly, squeezing her hand. She did not try and push me away. It was about one o'clock on a cold December afternoon: we had had an early lunch. I was still getting to know Caz. Her expressive brown eyes looked past me, over her shoulder, again. Most of her long blonde hair was concealed under a soft black hat. It used to belong to me. The hat, that is, not the hair. Though sometimes, I could do with some extra hair.

'I wonder you don't have gloves yourself,' she said.

'You know why. I don't feel the cold as you do.'

'Are you from another *planet*?'

'Just maybe I am.' Her breath fogged out past me as she looked nervously back the way we had come. It seemed to be getting dark, even so early in the afternoon. The sides of the cutting seemed oppressive, casting shadows.

'Do you remember,' she said hesitantly, 'what *he* said?'

'Who?' I said, my head still full of her smile, and my research the night before.

'The Brahan Seer, our local prophet, you idiot.'

'Oh. Him.'

'Yes. Him. 'I would not like to live when a black bridleless horse will pass through the Muir of Ord'.'

'Ah. What did he know?'

'He knew a lot, Donald. He may have seen that time is relative, that not all the things he foretold would happen at once. Natural shrewdness aside.'

'So… that may be why not everything he said came true in his own lifetime.' I had enjoyed watching her breath puff out as she spoke. I still held her hand. We went on a little way. There came the snap of a twig behind us. Caz turned sharply, pulling her hand from mine.

'What was that?'

'What, Caz?'

'*That!* That noise!'

'Probably just a stray dog.' I was thinking of the warm fire in my study, a toddy to drink, and more writing to do later.

'I don't know about you, but I haven't seen a single dog all the time we've been here. Not a cyclist, either. Isn't that strange?'

'It's the time of year. Cyclists don't want injuries in a place like this, so they stick to the roads.'

'What about the dogs, though?'

'I think they're hibernating.'

'Ha ha. Dogs are dogs, and they need *exercise*.'

I grew tired of her enquiry. 'Are you coming, or what?'

'I like to know where I'm going, though. Don't you?'

I stuck my hands in my jacket pockets, and carried on walking. I could hear her silence, stubborn and still, behind me for a while. I did not look back. Then, a long exhalation of breath. I smiled at the thought of her as a kind of stationary engine, not yet out of the shed. I sauntered on. Then I could hear her walking briskly to catch up.

'Donald. Wait up.' I slowed a little but did not stop. We were almost at a dilapidated bridge. The sky grumbled, and there was the smell of rain.

Caz looked up at the bridge, and the road somewhere beyond it, above our heads. 'Donald! I thought I saw a face…'

I smiled. 'It's that time of year…' I squinted up at the bridge myself.

Some of its girders had become quite rusted, giving it a dull orange sheen. One panel, most of its rivets gone, almost resembled a pouchy face, a little like a gargoyle, for a moment. I shook my head.

Reaching out, I took Caz's hand, pulling her nearer me, and in the same motion, both of us directly under the bridge. She looked surprised, then smiled. I rubbed her gloved hand attentively. She looked straight at me, then up at the underside of the bridge, her dark eyes showing a little bloodshot. Her breath came past me, vivid and warm. 'How long has it been since we first met?' she said softly.

'Yesterday.'

'Oh, I think it's been a wee bit longer than that.' I smiled, enjoying the aura of life that emanated from her. She reached over and kissed me. I held her. There was a slight rain whispering outside, rattling on the derelict roof of the bridge, falling through the joyless branches of the trees beyond, their arms outstretched like dark candelabra that no-one would ever light again. I held her a little while, and she pressed against me, so warm and vital. There was a long red streak of rust down one side of the bridge.

'Warmer now, Caz?'

'Oh, yes.'

'Will we go?'

'If we must.' I released her, perhaps before she was ready. She stumbled for a moment, and I caught her before she fell. 'Thanks.' She smiled. Caz ventured out onto the other side of the bridge, her voice echoing slightly. 'Look, it's snowing.'

'Nearly.' I joined her on the far side, and stood looking out onto the next part of the abandoned railway track for a moment. 'Kind of sleeting.' She shivered.

'Look, are you *sure* you don't need a hat?'

'I'm sure. I don't get cold easily.'

'Now, why is that?'

'I wish I knew. I could make a lot of money. The sooner we go, the sooner we'll be back. You sure you want to come?'

'Always, with you.' She sighed. I was fascinated by the longer puff of her breath, and the little cloud it created. I shielded my eyes with my bare hand, for a moment. The track wound on ahead of us. I stepped out first. Visibility was becoming reduced. The sleet was too thin to be true snow. Some of it settled on my jacket, my head. I did not mind. Caz stepped out after me, looking around her. I looked back at her. For a moment, a red face seemed to smile down at her out of the rusted ironwork, but it faded again.

Caz walked briskly to keep up with me. 'Do you think you've got enough for your book, Donald?'

'Nearly. I'll enjoy writing it up later.'

'I'm sure I'll enjoy reading it.'

'Good afternoon.' Caz shrieked. I almost did the same, drawing in my breath sharply. A red-cheeked, jovial man had joined us. His clothes seemed a little old-fashioned.

'Do you know much about the history of this line?' he asked. Caz was startled, staring at him.

'A little,' I said, more calmly. 'This was one of those lines closed by Dr Beeching.'

'He was after my time,' admitted the man, dressed in a kind of navy-coloured uniform. He puffed out his cheeks as he rolled along beside us: there was no other way to describe it. Perhaps he had once been in the Navy.

'Oh,' I said. 'Did you work on this line when it was still running?'

'I did indeed sir, surely as my name is Jack.'

'Really? Do tell us about it.' Caz had stood stock still since his sudden appearance. She now walked a little way behind. 'Caz,' I said, without turning around. 'Come and join us.'

'Donald.' She spoke softly. 'I think we should go home.'

'We *are* going home, Caz. Just a longer way round.'

'Are we?'

Now it was the turn of the old railwayman to stand very still. Then he reached out his hand, slapped his pockets. He took a few moments to search for something. Caz watched him intently, her eyes flicking back and forth between him and me. He eventually found an old, blackened pipe of a kind I had not seen since my grandfather's generation, and some matches.

'Tell us,' I said again, quietly. A slow smile spread across his face. Jack puffed out his cheeks again. A brief strike of the match illuminated his face, shadows forming under his eyes. His hands seemed curiously blackened. He stood completely still, as the first tendril of smoke wafted from his pipe. Then he began to move, very slowly. We had to slow right down to keep pace with him.

Caz maintained her distance from him still. She looked over her shoulder, back at the rusted bridge. Then she sighed, her breath fogging conspicuously as she did so, and followed the railwayman and me along the track, leading away from Fortrose, towards Avoch, another Black Isle village, north and east of Inverness.

'This is where Rosehaugh stood,' said Jack, his pipe clamped between his teeth, staring straight ahead into the sleet, as if defying it to harm him. 'The big house… did you know about that… 'foolish pride without sense will put in the place of the seed of the deer the seed of the goat, and the beautiful Black Isle will fall under the management of the fishermen of Avoch'.'

Caz quickened her pace, and came closer to me, yet still further from Jack. 'Donald,' she hissed. 'What does he *mean*? I don't like this.'

'It's like you were saying earlier. The Brahan Seer could see round a few corners, he was well known for it… pity he didn't foresee his own death. The Rosehaugh estate came to be managed by the Fletchers, whose symbol is the goat, rather than the long-standing Mackenzies, with their badge of the deer, or *caberfeidh*. Another prophecy fulfilled.'

The sleet continued to drive into our faces, yet Jack's pace seemed to pick up speed a little. His breath, when I could see it, seemed so much darker than Caz's, nearly as thick as the smoke from his pipe. He must have been smoking for a long time. I shuddered to think of the state of his lungs. He moved a little more quickly. The smoke spiralled out of his pipe, and over his shoulder, leaving a column of it behind. Caz stepped deliberately out of its path, as it lingered in the air.

'Don!' she hissed again. 'Do we *really* have to…' she jerked her head in his direction. I smiled at her. She was not reassured. I took hold of her hand, and squeezed tight. I brought her up alongside Jack, with me in the middle, and her at the edge of the track, to the left. Jack's eyes seemed to follow us, even though he remained where he was, trudging straight ahead.

Caz addressed him for the first time. 'Er, was the weather often like this when you worked on the line?' The column of smoke from his pipe appeared to grow thicker as she spoke. His face grew redder, too.

'Soldiers will come from Tarradale on a chariot without horse or bridle which will leave the Muir of Ord a wilderness,' he replied, still staring determinedly ahead of him.

'What?' she said, turning to me. 'What does he mean? Does he mean- the weather? Oh Don, I want to go home.'

'We are,' I replied levelly.

'It's getting so cold,' she said. 'And still no-one else is walking out this way.'

'It's that time of year,' I said briskly. She looked at me.

'You're a strange one.'

'Oh, I know. I love it out here.' We still kept pace with Jack, however unwillingly.

'If this line could be saved,' I said to Jack, 'would you do it now?'

'What do you mean?' said Caz sharply. 'This line was lost close to 50 years ago.'

Jack smiled, and seemed to take up more room than he had before. Perhaps it was an effect of the failing light. The sleet lay in a trail behind us, like ball bearings. Ahead of us, improbably, the track was clear. Jack walked a little faster, humming to himself.

Some distance ahead, I could perceive the mouth of a tunnel I had not seen before, and which I could not recall seeing marked on any map. Jack seemed more squat than ever, and there was increasingly less elbow-room beside him. His uniform was black now; perhaps it had always been so, and I had just mistaken it for navy earlier. A dim red glow seemed to come from his chest, but I knew it must surely come from his pipe. He moved faster still.

'What's the rush?' I enquired. 'Have you a train to catch?' It seemed as if none of us had the freedom to stop moving of our own accord.

'Och no,' he chuckled, 'that was over *long* ago.' We were drawn along beside him, almost rattling along. His pipe smoke grew yet blacker and thicker, passing behind him and around him, making us cough.

'Where are we *going*?' demanded Caz as we followed him. The long tunnel loomed up ahead.

'To the Muir of Ord,' he replied in a deeper voice, that had a rattle in it. 'The trains used to come from there, over this way, you know. There was no direct route from Inverness by road then. For some of us, the trains *never* stopped coming this way.'

'No!' she shouted. I tried to slow down, but our feet kept pace beside him. Jack's arms grew thicker still. The trees seemed to move a little towards us from either side of the track. Jack's feet moved faster, in a rhythm we could only imitate, drawn along just behind him. He was fast becoming a moving, breathing, chattering *thing* that was the more horrible for the remainder of its human substance. The transformed railwayman threw back his head and *screeched* as we approached the tunnel. His head had become a long swollen funnel with teeth, that turned and leered at us. For some time now, I have had the opportunity to reflect on the words: 'I would not like to live when a black bridleless horse shall pass through the Muir of Ord.'

An Island Of Talking Heads

Caligulus Minus shivered as he boarded the trireme floating off the Gaulish coast. He looked back at the shore. 'I don't like it,' he said to Sextus Paulus, standing next in line to him.

'We're not paid to like it,' said Paulus shortly, looking straight ahead of him. 'Emperor Claudius is sending us, it must be the will of the gods.' Minus looked at the dark, heaving water beyond them. The open sea was a strange, hostile force to him. He had seen little of it in his lifetime. The elements had their own spaces, and should be respected. Earth; fire; air; water. The god of water would be displeased. He seemed angry indeed as the trireme rocked to and fro. Minus said a silent prayer for a safe homecoming as he boarded, apprehensive, carrying his pack and spear. The long decks stretched below them like a wide empty mouth, the rowlocks awaiting like teeth for a meal. Minus walked to his place, again behind Paulus, stowed his kit and awaited the order to begin rowing. The centurion marched up and down the centre as the rowing positions were filled.

'Stand by!' he barked. 'Prepare to depart!' Minus comforted himself with the familiar procedure, taking orders. This was surely no different to other missions the Ninth had undertaken. But perhaps Neptune would still be angry. The invasion under Divine Julius had failed, after all. His hand shook as he grasped the oar. It was good, firm carpentry, shaped by Roman hands. The galley filled up, and they prepared to cast off. Minus felt better as they began to move with the tide, in and out, in and out, to the beat of the drum. In front of him, it was Paulus who looked anxious, prone to seasickness.

'I've heard such things,' he whispered under his breath. 'the people of this island are such barbarians! They sacrifice on the wrong days, and I heard from my uncle here in Gaul, who traded with some of them, they have riches in their burials…'

'Riches?' Minus looked interested for the first time, keeping the rhythm, and out of range of the centurion's eye.

'Yes, but not as we use them. I heard… of sacrificial totems, of things worshipped after they are dead, of stones with holes in their heads, heads that talk after they are dead.'

'After death?'

'Yes. They are… unholy relics. Their ancestors never leave them in peace.' Minus thought as he rowed, flexing his large muscles. Perhaps his ancestors would travel with him, to the treasure, to this island of talking heads.

Flowers At A Grave

'Oh, look, there are flowers at his grave,' said my aunt dismissively, suddenly reaching for her handkerchief. We stood in the graveyard, on a bright May day. The shadows of the graves loomed black and solid across the grass. Some graves were covered in flowers; some new, some withered. One stone had blue football scarves and regalia. One had political slogans.

The one we were examining was plain, upright, granite, much like the person whose life it commemorated. He had had a stormy crossing, a remarkable journey, now over, now at peace. It seemed someone else, apart from his family and his church, had chosen to remember him, too. It was a strong part of our background, with the emphasis so much on the next world, that flowers are inappropriate at a grave. Now, in defiance of this ban, there was a bouquet of flowers at the grave. It was a very small bouquet, already wilting in the sun, but it broke the even lines of the grass and the granite, the stems like plaintive fingers, reaching up to the silent stone.

There was no need to speak. My aunt might have disdained the flowers out of habit or from conviction. But the fact was, we were there, bringing flowers with our thoughts.

Happy Death Men

'Have ye got it?' MacNeil emerged from behind a gravestone, lugging a form only too like himself, wrapped in coarse sacking. The Edinburgh scene was lit by only a sliver of moon. The lamplight in the adjacent street flickered.

'Aye. Come on, let's go.'

'Wait, wait. Is it the one?'

'We're all the same here. I mean, they are.'

'Yer forgetting yerself.' Richardson moved to grasp the limp shape by the feet, and concentrated on moving through the graveyard: they were on a timetable. The fitful light from the street by the church showed the dark stain of the ground, forced like a lock. MacNeil found it hard to take his eyes off it, still in his line of sight as he backed towards the cemetery gate, the head of the body in his care lolling from side to side. The arms, which had been pressed together in a serene pose, flopped apart, trailing on the ground and seeming to claw at MacNeil in passing. He jumped, almost dropping their charge. Richardson glared. 'Get a grip.'

'The Professor should be waiting. Soup and bread, he said-' MacNeil negotiated a rough tussock in the older part of the cemetery, and nearly tripped, looking behind him towards the gate.

'Shut it. He promised money, that's all we need.' The figure between them seemed reluctant to leave, one of the hands catching in a briar bush and tugging at the thorny stems. Richardson swore under his breath, and released his end. MacNeil did likewise, mopping his brow and crossing himself, looking around in fear. 'Stop that,' snarled the other. 'You know it's no good. Well- get on with it, then!'

MacNeil bent over, reluctant for such direct contact. He pulled the sleeve of his overcoat over his hand, and untangled the stiff, unrelenting fingers from the bush. He looked up briefly to check the rest of their path was clear. 'We havena all night!' he was reminded. They picked up the pace again, and emerged onto the cobbled street of the Cowgate. MacNeil was clearly relieved as they tipped the body into a small handcart, and covered it over. The wheels creaked slightly as they set off for the back door of the hospital. A bare arm flopped out again, unseen by them in their haste. It seemed to be pointing back at the graveyard.

Let Her Go Down

The tide runs at me. This is the end. The old lady beneath me shudders. I instructed the crew to abandon ship some time ago. There is no-one else here, just her and me. Nothing else can be done for her, I know. Unless I leave now, I will go down with her, but part of me still clings to hope as I cling to the mast. It is so hard to let go. I was proud of her. It is hard to put into words the love of this vessel, what she meant to her builders, to the crew, to me. I still feel something, even when the aft mast is gone, and her decks below gape. This ship is returning inexorably to the ocean, I cannot stop it, yet somehow I want to, by staying on. She will take me with her, if I stay too long. Drowning is not romantic. I have seen the faces of men dragged back from the water, too late to save them, made almost more water than flesh. The deck tilts further forward, the timbers screaming. She was built in Dundee, in a time now gone. I am her leader, the captain privileged to be at her death. This is no longer the ship I knew. I am clutching at memories, and increasingly to the grey shroud that comes rushing at me, that will close over my head before I know it. It is a kindness that these great torn sides will not see daylight again, that they go down to their grave. She shifts again on the rocks, the storm pushing her further to her doom. She is stripped of her honour, the memories, already a wreck with no fit place or purpose above water. I am grieving, but the water will take me if I do not act now. I turn, fling off my uniform and dive into the tide, hoping to avoid the rocks, hoping for life.

Lighthouse

I put the body in the corner. It was only decent. He was my friend. Or he was, before we argued. I found hammer and nails, and prepared a coffin. I had many skills, before the Mice came for me. They gnaw and they gnaw, and I cannot get warm. Never never. It is so cold here, on this blasted rock. Literally. The wind blows under the foundations, here we stand and face the rain… stood on stilts, in the teeth of the storms. It is thirty years since the King lost us America. I wish I had tea here, another means to keep warm. The light from my oil lamp casts shadows, and I fear the Mice will come back again.

In the corner is… It, the thing that used to be He. Griffiths, as was. I am Powell. I always will be. No power on Earth can take that from me. I write this letter by the lantern light… that is my salvation. The shadows leer and stretch and I feel their fingers on my back… crawling.

We had our differences, right enough. Put two grown men on a rock like this Smalls Lighthouse, and they will pick at each other over something. But now I fear, I fear my righteous conduct will not be recognised, and he must be kept secret.

***

I have prepared his little house, a sacred ark to take him away in the rising flood. The rain is lashing this trap, this prison, this house of God. I must… take him outside, welcome the elements. Those who read this will come, and I would have them know the truth. He must be in his house, to welcome them.

I struggle outside, resisting the wind, out on the gallery, where the great light still flashes. It glares on me as a great eye, while I try to do what is right. The only way. I have put his house outside of mine. I lash it with ropes, and trust to God. I retreat to my righteous prison. I hold the lamp, and watch the shadows. Then, there is a shift. A thump. The dreadful door of the little house I built opens, and the figure inside shifts, it points, as he did in life. It accuses forever. I am white, I am a statue, I may never move again.

After The Funeral

I stumble away from the graveside, with the support of my friend. We walk towards the gate in the churchyard, under a louring November sky. 'I'll never forget her,' I say, my breath coming in starts. That raw rectangle of earth and the box we had just put in it didn't seem to be real. She is still with me, regardless. Even death can't stop her. Typical. My breath comes in dry heaves, like the urge to be sick. My friend watches, black-clothed and sympathetic. 'I'll sit down,' I say, finding a bench. The words come out fast. 'There was nobody like her. Nobody. Never again.' My friend stays silent. I look up at the sky, the way the evening comes on too soon, the remorseless tide of black chasing away the light. After the time change at the end of October, the light really loses the will to live for a while, a fading battle, retreating into December and the shortest day. It has to be propped up by Christmas lights and other garish things I do not want to think of today. I see two stars in a fading patch of blue, surrounded by the dark. It is closing on them fast. I look up, engrossed in the drama. I blink, and they are gone, then still there, all the brighter, against the dark. I remember this day, when two stars sang together.

Loch Leven

Such idolatrous nonsense. Still she holds onto this pretence after her disgrace, as a fallen queen. Flowers in the dirt. I detest her popish practices, her litany, her superstition. It is against the law and purpose of Scotland. She sews, she eats, she prays to idols, all on a scale to show her former estate. She costs the government enough. She beseeches me with her eyes, her voice still half-French from her raising and her first marriage. 'Ah Misteer Douglas, I would another blanket,' always for more than we can afford. She is supposed to think over her sins here, her presumption, her breaking of the law. The walls preach reconciliation, the limited space her exclusion from God's elect, if only she would listen.

Yet there are days when I sense her kindness to me. Her eyes open wide, she asks after my sister's children, how are the dogs in the kitchen today? I see the light through the window illuminate her figure, how fine it is. She says she would like to have more children. The golden light covers her, it seems natural. Is it right to keep such a royal bird in this cage. I will talk to her about it. Perhaps I will fly with her.

Moon Dance

We achieved blast-off at 08.15 hours EST. We drove from Jacksonville down to Cape Kennedy, in Florida. We were well provisioned on the remains of what she called 'a very talkative cake' I had made for her birthday. I stroked her bare right arm, and held her hand briefly. It is safe to do that in an automatic. She had not been there in a long time, not since a little girl, shortly before the moon landing. I snapped her on Launch Bay 39. Over her shoulder, you could see the launching point for some of the former space shuttles, retired that year, 2011. It was also where the *Challenger* exploded, shortly after its launch in January 1986. It was a warmer October than I was used to, yet with cool breezes blowing in off the sea. There were alligators in pools nearby, the first time I had ever seen one. The moon hung low in the sky, clearly visible in the afternoon. A source of dreams, not just the American Dream, though clearly they tied theirs into reaching the Moon first, in little nibbles then increasingly larger bites until swallowing it into conquest in July 1969. I thought I could see the Sea of Nectar. My princess and I made our way through the complex. We saw the actual Launch Control from 1969, now literally a museum piece. The Apollo V hung hugely over our heads in an exhibit, shadowing everything else in the hangar. 1960s spacesuits stood eerie as dummies, their gloved hands outstretched. I leaned over and grasped her hand, sitting next to her on the tour bus. She relaxed, her fingers closing around mine. We did lunch in small instalments, chiefly pieces of fruit. I looked at the crisp slices of apple, and wished I could have saved her from some of her choices, in a former life. She had to be her own woman, though, and free. With me in her life, she was waking from the evil spell of the past. She read on how astronauts tend to lose weight in space. 'That's what I need to do,' she said wryly, brushing her hair back. I held her hand.

'Silly girl,' I said gently. 'Whatever for? I think-' but she didn't let me finish. She kissed me, our lips meeting and making one round full moon.

Scramble

I keep her picture here, in my wallet. My American girl. Not so much a GI Jane as a filing clerk, who came in with the Yanks. There she is, in her uniform, smiling just for me. Beautiful. The others admire her, even as they tease me. Here in Kinloss, on the Moray Firth, we have to be ready at any time. When that siren pulls us out of bed, we have to be ready for Hitler.

There was a Cistercian monastery here, before the Reformation. We went walking in the ruins, and it was there I proposed to her. We'd only known each other a month, but you never know, with a war on… seize the moment! The evening light filtered through the Gothic window, red fingers lighting on her face. It made me think of the bars on a convent. We walked her little dog on the beach. I'd been to the jeweller's in Elgin for the ring. It sparkled in the sunset as I put it on her, and kissed her. The red light fell over me too.

I live every day for her. She seems so happy. We are so happy. A quiet ceremony, next month, in December, in a small parish church in Elgin. My mother's coming up from Aberdeen. I've booked my leave. Grand times, even if it's just going to be two days in a cottage. We can go walking. Her little dog always needs walking, anyway.

I take out my wallet again. How did I get so lucky? I was just a librarian before the war, not much more than a clerk. So we have that in common. She was so natural, less reserve than one of our girls. I liked that about her: a straight-talker.

We sit smoking in the mess, waiting. Chess sets are out, card games abound, but everyone here is watching and waiting. Then it comes: the doleful hooting of the siren. Games are abandoned at a moment's notice, cigarettes stubbed out in ashtrays, pipes emptied abruptly. I grab my harness at the door and buckle it on as I run towards the 'kite'. I run towards her, towering above us like a castle. I am the pilot. I take my position, and prop her picture above the instruments. The others smile as we prepare for take-off. Nothing can separate her and me.

Sea Henge

The sea is where one life ends. The life of the land surrenders to the sea, is taken over and rinsed out into the tide, the endless horizon. When the chief of this Neolithic tribe died, his people were workers in wood as well as stone. They took their time, cutting down a great oak with their tools, dragging it close to the sea and burying it upside-down. The coastline has changed since then, of course. It was in view of the sea then: now it is almost in the sea itself. The tide coming further back than usual was a vagary of the spring tides, revealing the upended stem and the wooden stumps surrounding it like members of a congregation, their heads bowed in respect for his journey to the next life. Anyone who steps inside the circle can feel this. All things pass away: this monument, and its surrounding circle, are diminished by the passing of time. The experts come, and murmur and analyse, and build a modern replica. They talk about authenticity. They think it may be a fertility symbol. The long-long-dead remains of the ancient people would laugh. They are part of the very sand that erodes their monument, now.

New Kid On The Breeze Block

Mel Gibson's face stared out of a poster over the foyer of the MacRobert Centre, at the University of Stirling. The would-be Guardian of Scotland's expression did not alter as a slightly-built girl fought her way through the large, stiff doors at the entrance, one of them catching her shoulder as she went through. She winced and rubbed it, her bag slipping from her shoulder to the floor. She bent to pick it up, thinking sour thoughts of the architect.

Heather made her way through the car park outside towards her first English lecture in the Cottrell Building. She sat up at the back of the modern theatre, as she did at the cinema, an independent figure, chewing a pen and looking around her at the multitude. 'You don't want to go to Oxford,' said the lecturer when she had started discussing *Peter and the Wolf*. Heather smiled and agreed for her own reasons.

After the lecture, she left the same solitary figure who arrived: little contact with others, but always watching them, inferring, calculating, believing. It had started to rain. Her arms folded, she crossed over beneath the walkway over the carpark, smiling at the sign warning drivers about ducks. The student newspaper had been quick to point out, tongue in cheek, this implied ducks were more important than students. As if on cue, there came the sound of quacking from the direction of Airthrey Pond. Heather walked through the building, past the on-campus bookshop, travel agent, chemist and newsagent then outside to the bridge spanning Airthrey Pond.

It was officially designated a man-made loch, but she defined it as a large pond. She always had her own definitions. The rain splashed gently on the water below. She had heard tales of the things lurking below the surface, relics of student parties and other less cheerful occasions. She strained her eyes to see if there were a trace of the Mini Cooper a friend of a relative had told her about, but if it was there, or had ever been, she could not see. She walked on, the floodlights at either end of the bridge illuminating the dull afternoon. The halls of residence loomed ever closer, their design reminding her of a shoebox city of Jericho she had once made in Sunday School. She took a left turn after the bridge to get to her hall, known by the acronym ASH.

She appreciated the warmth on entering the foyer, rubbing her arms briefly. Walking down the corridor, the Wallace Monument was strongly visible through the window, lit up in orange like a rocket. Heather paused to wipe her steamed-up glasses with the cuff of her sleeve. Now she could make out the finer details of the building. Long ago she had visited it, aged seven.

Down the five flights of steps to her room on the first floor. A sigh of relief as she was free of the pressures of others, their expectations of conversation, their ideas, their behaviour. She told no-one about her medication, or the meaning of her visits to the psychology block when she did not study science. Sometimes she still felt a false guilt.

Heather's room was furnished simply. The large breeze blocks comprising the walls seemed white and uncompromising. She had started to reform the starkness, a picture of a Volkswagen Beetle in psychedelic colours on one wall, the Blues Brothers on another. She lay back on the bed and thought about her English essay, an 'attempt at a sympathetic explanation' of a Gertrude Stein story. Farmers and eggs and cows, oh my. Philosophy was taught so badly, she vowed to ditch it as soon as possible.

Tea was a simple matter of some pasta, or would have been had she been able to access the kitchen with a single cooker to share between fourteen people, the first and second floors combined. Sometimes it wasn't possible to eat before ten o'clock at night. She improvised with a Mars Bar, and the associated guilt.

Heather went home for her twenty-first birthday. She celebrated it quietly over a weekend, came back and got on with her studies. The days shortened. She did not read newspapers often, but enjoyed an article on Noah Webster's first dictionary of American English, published in 1836. Some day her own poetry would be recognised. She happily devoured the novel a week required for her English tutorials. The nine weeks' Christmas holidays were coming soon.

***

Tuesday, 12th March 1996. Heather smiled at some of her hallmates, preparing for a pyjama party. The snow had fallen between her English and History classes. Snowmen were being built outside the MacRobert Centre, and the halls. She had recently been to see a performance of *Animal Farm* in the former, and had especially enjoyed the bagpipes when the windmill collapsed. Her friends sounded happy, making plans for flat sharing in second year. She made no such commitment, but was glad to be better, off the medication.

The following morning, she was off campus in town, shopping, and came back on the number 53 bus around 12 noon. There was a great stillness in the air as she got off the bus. The University flag was flying at half mast. Heather went towards the bookshop, changed her mind and walked to the Chaplaincy, placed incongruously close to the student bars. She had never been there before, but she knew some students who went there regularly, and it seemed a likely place from which to get news.

No-one seemed inclined to talk when she entered, a reporter's voice on the radio in the corner doing so instead, trying to impart compassion to a terrible event. It was not so far away, Heather thought, just three miles, so she had heard. She did not know what to feel. She learned the essentials of what had happened, and left. She walked out into the snow, now beginning to melt. The ice on the pond was cracking.

She talked to the ducks, to tell them what was wrong. They quacked and spread their wings and ignored her. One of the surviving snowmen was half melted, his smile lop-sided. She wished he were as intact as the day before. She returned to ASH, and scribbled frantically in her notebook until the point of her pencil broke.

After the numbness wore off, there were repercussions. She began to go back into the old downward spiral. The need to punish herself, thinking of standing in the pond.

Hold on, she thought. To the next cup of tea. One step at a time. English classes were still quite enjoyable: she read the part of Cecily in *The Importance of Being Earnest*, and discovered Emily Dickinson's comforting morbidity. She returned to the doctors' on-site general practice. But the medicine wasn't working as before, firing the synapses. Like building a fire in an igloo in her head.

Life grew less real. She was uncertain as to whether to return next year. Heather felt afraid, claustrophobic, lacking co-ordination. She gave up on the effort involved in preparing pasta, and ate sandwiches. She went on holiday with her parents to Pitlochry for a week at Easter, eating chocolate and watching repeats of *The Avengers.* She explained it to her mother as 'a very psychological drama'.

      The lengthening days and warmer weather as April passed seemed undeserved at Stirling, as if time should have stopped in mid-March. Heather saw dark things under the bed, like when she was a wee child in the north, with wolves at the back of her wardrobe. She looked up to Jake and Elwood in every sense. 'You know what?' she whispered to them on the night before her English exam. There was no putting it off, no denying it, even with a doctor's note: the authorities were implacable. 'I'm putting the band back together.' She put on a pair of sunglasses, and laughed hysterically at herself in a mirror. Heather looked at the pills by her bedside. She squeezed her eyes tight shut. She sat on the edge of her bed, rocking back and forth. From a distance, down a tunnel far away, she heard the urgent voice of James Brown, so full of energy. 'Do you see the light?'

Martyrdom

They took her to the water, the wind blowing in their faces. This was the authority of King Charles II being enforced: bringing those obstinate Presbyterians to heel. Young Margaret could smell the salt of the sea, near her home on the Solway, where she had lived her eighteen years. It was so familiar. The tide ran strongly here.

Elaine was struggling. She had had this problem before leaving school, her knowledge that she was too fat. No-one else could see it: no-one else cared. She alone could diagnose and cure it. She was proud of that, sometimes. She was a psychology student, after all.

Young Margaret was led down onto the estuary of the Solway, with the elder Margaret. They would not let the King have his way. Who were they, to stand up to him? 'Only women,' said one soldier, laughing as he tied the elder Margaret to the stake. The tide was out, but already it was starting to turn. Even the soldiers feared it.

Elaine had to face facts. She had to get in shape, join the gym. Living in halls, she stole ice-cream from another girl on the same floor. Elaine knew she was doing her a favour. She never bought that kind of food herself, never. Too many calories. No-one saw her coming out of the toilet at midnight, wiping her mouth. Her friends would ask her why her throat was so sore the next day, and she would just shrug and say, 'I've got a frog in my throat,' and banish all thoughts of cream cakes. Until later.

Young Margaret watched the tide coming in. All her life, she had lived here near the Solway, where her parents had taught her about God. The elder Margaret's clothes were catching in the rising tide, getting heavier. She was singing the Psalms. The soldiers watched from the safe distance of the bank.

Elaine was enjoying the term. She was learning, she was taking exercise, she had nice new clothes. The midnight episodes were occasional abnormalities, under her control. No-one knew what she did. It was only right she edit out the excess. She had to measure up, practice what she learned. She wanted to be the best.

The elder Margaret was not singing now. Young Margaret could just see her grey hair, bobbing above the water, further down the estuary. She was already in another world. The water made its own song, lapping at her feet.

Elaine was good with problems, good with ideas. She listened to her friends, cared about them, studied them, analysed them. She was pleased with her progress, pleased at everything going so well at sunny Stirling University. Her clothes were great, her face was not too bad… but there was still the need for discipline, sometimes.

Margaret felt the tug of the water around her waist. It was cold, a penetrating chill to the bone. She was tied firm to the stake, hands lashed to her sides. She was losing the feeling in her hands. The tide tugged at her. She would never have a husband, never know what it was to bring forth a child. The water was coming for her, coloured all shades of grey. She could not see the other Margaret's head now. She had had her chance. Young Margaret would not, in her turn, recant, not let the Presbyterian Kirk be run by lairds or by the King, by none other than her Lord Jesus. She knew whom she had believed.

The autumn semester was getting on. Elaine was happy. Her grades were not what she had hoped for at the start, but they were good enough. She would get there. But how could she practise as a psychologist if she was *fundamentally too fat?* She had to show by example, she was strong and disciplined. She kept on top of things. And still, her wicked face did not show the benefits of her hard, hard work. She knew the boys did not want her as she was. Sure, one *had* asked her out, but he could not be serious. He would have to wait until she was better. *Much* better.

Margaret felt the pressure on her chest. The tide was a lover, folding her closer and closer. 'Strong bulls of Bashan me surround.' That came back to her, from the Psalms. The soldiers watched. They had been shouting earlier, now they were silent. Not out of respect, just watching. Waiting. Their time was coming. Hers was slipping away. The sands of time were sinking beneath her feet, long gone stone cold. The cold was seeping into her every fibre, but she still fought to hold onto praise, her personal victory, her dignity. She heard the Psalms in the water.

Elaine found it harder to hold a pen in class. She collapsed in her last exam of the semester, held in the indoor tennis court, symbol of all she aspired to. She was rushed to hospital in an ambulance, a saline drip in her arm. She looked up at it, thought of the bubbles floating in it like lemonade, pumping fat into her arm. She screamed, and ripped it out. The paramedic held her arm and tried to replace it. It was so hard to find a vein in that stick-like, scarecrow arm.

Margaret held her chin up. She looked calmly at the soldiers. She was above them in every way that mattered. The tide was coming, the force of nature having its way. Her long, bedraggled hair was floating behind her like a train. In years to come, one of these soldiers would die of thirst. Margaret looked up, up, at the hills beyond her home. 'I to the hills will lift mine eyes. From whence doth come mine aid?

We Are For The Dark

The rays of the setting sun fell over the shrine of Columba. Brother Peter looked up from his garden, moved as he often was by the simplicity of the stone cell, on which their own were based. The cluster of wooden buildings near him resembled a beehive, the swarm of monks inside full of a collective industry.

Peter was a practical man, who enjoyed the physical aspects of monastic life. He hoed the ground of the fennel bed in front of him, turning the ground over, moist and fertile. He was used to toiling in the fields beyond the enclave, sweat pouring onto his habit. Before this life, he had been used to rougher work still, out on the pounding waves of the coast of Dalriada (Dalriada was an ancient western kingdom in Scotland, covering Argyll), rowing and sailing and catching and cursing on many a stormy night.

But God had laid his hand on him, and drawn him to Iona. A retreat from the world of men it may be, but a very hard and demanding life, still, more pleasing to him than the way he had been. His wife had died the winter of the famine, and if it were not for God, he himself would likely have drowned from carelessness or grief or drunkenness.

Peter paused, looking out to sea. The pain of that wound would never quite heal; it rose and fell like the tide on the white sandy bay, soft and pure. There were green pebbles there, said to be the tears of St Columba, or Columcille. Peter had had many tears, lost in the sea.

The wind ruffled his hair. Instinctively he bowed towards the shrine, though it was not three hours since he had last been there. He bent his back to the rhythm of the hoe, moving on to the beds of sorrel and mint. Some were used in Markus the Brother Hospitaller's physic to cure the sick. That and prayer were their remedies.

Sometimes Peter wished he had their skill, the healers. He identified more with the potters: the wheel moving in its orbit, how he knew he was an unworthy vessel, cracked and ugly in its coarse body, yet filled and used. He was a thing of the earth, brown and shapeless. He winced when the pots got dropped, or smashed. As if they carried a part of his soul.

Peter turned his back to the sea as he continued weeding. Ahead rose the hill of Dun Bhuirg, the remains of ancient fortifications frowning down from the crest. One of several wooden crosses on the island was positioned at his right, and to his left there was St Martin's Cross, built of stone, one of the first High Crosses. The ring around the arms cast a long shadow. It marked the entrance to the shrine of Columcille. A series of wooden crosses led from there down to the bay, by the Street of the Dead, past the royal burial ground, the Reilig Odhrain, to the bay. The route marked a simple pilgrimage. Peter had done that and more, walking around the entire island.

Brother Colm emerged from one of the simple wooden buildings as the chapel bell began to toll for evening prayers. The chapel was named after St Michael. They would need the Archangel's protection against more than storms if certain rumours were to be believed. Peter rested on his hoe. The sunset was lighting up the bay in red.

'Come,' said Colm, a recent addition to the brotherhood, from a wealthy family. He was used to having his way in most things. Peter smiled, and bowed ironically. They proceeded past the shrine and the refectory, into the Chapel of St Michael, a simple oblong building.

A comforting glow came from the candles, already lit for the service. Their fellow Brothers were lined in two rows before the basic wooden altar, the Precentor Duncan at its head. Seeing they were all present, he began to sing the first line of Psalm 51. The others responded.

As before, Peter focussed on his surroundings as a means to lift his thoughts. He felt a brief regret he was not better at singing. The light through the small window facing him was fading now over the sea, scarlet fingers stretching inside the Chapel and lighting on the far wall. It touched Peter's shoulder.

He sang in Latin for the forgiveness of a sinful life, purified with hyssop, may the Spirit of the Lord not be taken from him. He looked up at the stylised image of the dove carved above the altar, the traditional likeness of the Holy Spirit. He remembered he should be concentrating on singing, and returned his attention to the floor, a rough earthen surface not much different to how it was when Columba landed.

Peter's recent order to transcribe part of the Book of Kells had filled him with fear. He had rough, chapped, untaught hands for such a thing of beauty. The only teaching he had had in his life had been since he had arrived on Iona. His knowledge of the meaning of the words and symbols was very recent, and he did not entirely understand either yet. He had been afraid of spoiling the delicate work the others had already done. Yet he had to copy the page of the first chapter of St John, with its talk of the Word and the life, and the words that brought life. Some of that he understood from his background, the sea a bitter grave for many of his family. He had sat in an isolated wooden cubicle writing in the Book while others were at the chapter house, listening to the Rule, wishing he could join them.

Peter sensed the Psalm coming to an end, his conditioned responses echoing from him like a voice in one of the caves over on the west side. He exchanged a wry glance with Colm. He sensed the Abbot's eyes on them, and straightened like a soldier. The assembled monks dispersed to their dormitory for the night, apart from the chosen night watchman.

Peter's head had barely touched his pallet than Colm was shaking him by the shoulder. 'Rise,' he said imperiously, 'we have a visitor!' Peter restrained what remained of his fisherman's language and rubbed his eyes, stretching as he rose.

He followed Colm's retreating back out of the dormitory towards the infirmary, which completed the quadrangle of buildings. Within lay a half-naked man, soaked and shivering. He had one wound, which bled slowly, and many bruises, tended by the Brother Hospitaller, Markus. The stranger seemed very afraid. '*They* came,' he said, staring intently at the ceiling. 'Too many. God help us.'

Colm turned to Peter, shocked. There had been no Norse incursions for several years. As if by common consent, they walked over to an alcove in the infirmary, which was said to be blessed by Columba himself. They knelt. 'Hear us, oh hear us, hear us,' said Colm, his teeth chattering. He drew a deep breath and said, without looking at Peter, 'Do you think he speaks truth? He may be foolish, lost, not knowing what he says.' Peter nodded fervently: how he wanted to believe it. He closed his eyes, prayed hard in silence and rose, leaving Colm a little reassured, watching him out of the corner of his eye.

Peter went over and sat near the stranger. 'God be praised you were not drowned,' he said carefully, looking out at the night view through the arched window in the wall nearby. It was pitch dark save for candles burning near them. Markus was applying his remedies to the man's body, some of it derived from the plants in the garden. Peter almost smiled to see the application of his earlier work. Markus was known to be under a vow of silence at present: perhaps that was why Colm had fetched him.

'Where were you bound?' said Peter, still not looking at the stranger directly. He did not like the man's eyes. That kind of fear could be contagious. 'I was in the fishing trade before God called me.' The stranger seemed to relax a little. Markus finished rubbing on the unguent he had prepared from his stores, tied some bandages over the man's chest and offered him a spare robe. The worst wound had stopped bleeding.

'I drifted far, Brother. The storm took me, but it also saved me... from *them*. God be praised.'

'If he has spared you to warn us, God be praised indeed. You saw... some others?' The strange man nodded, clutching the proffered robe and pulling it over his head. In the corner, Colm kept wiping his sweating hands.

'I am Thomas,' he said. 'My father... they burnt his homestead on Mull. Nothing... but desolation.' His voice cracked and he spat on the infirmary floor before remembering where he was, and rubbed his mouth with the edge of the sleeve. He slumped back onto the pallet, staring up at the ceiling, seeming hardly alive. Markus pointed to the door. Peter and Colm returned without a word to the dormitory, and their cubicles. Peter gazed up at the timbered roof, and closed his eyes.

There was the usual ringing of the bell for the first prayers of the day, at which Peter sighed and rose again. Around him, things had changed. Great stone arches towered up around him, vast and unreachable as a lost treasure. No-one else was present. He pushed at a heavy oak door, descending the steps to cloisters, great stone enclaves of a very grand abbey that seemed too high for him in every sense.

He had little time to wonder: he was moving like something on the potter's wheel, beyond his own will or strength. He ran down the Street of the Dead to the bay, and started praying hard for deliverance. He knelt on the sand, was filled with awe at the majesty of God in his surroundings, surely his people were safe here. History was here in power, with memories of Columba. Stone arches rose out of the sand beside him, and grew to frame the sky like great grey clouds.

Hills, ruins, old crofts, a chapel, sheep, behind him. 'The Lord is my shepherd.' Peter felt some small stones through his coarse robe, as well as the sand. He was glad: wanted to stay awake, to prevent the imminent threat through prayer. He could see over to Ireland. The sea burst into fire. Fire on the water. It moved from the sea, and settled on his head. It did not burn him: it flickered with a curious gentleness. He knew it was the sign of the dove, as if he could understand everything for one precious watch of the clock.

He looked out to sea, took in the regular rhythm of the feared prows, and his heart burned with pity. Bloodthirsty men within the ships, united in purpose, launched out in organised chaos to destroy his little world. Peter wished he could reach out to them, even be the means of healing them, of their lust for gold and land. Amen and Amen. They were moving very fast towards him, over the sea, a sea made of glass, murder and pain in their eyes. He knew they longed to be forgiven. Peter stood up, alone on the beach. He was unafraid.

They were massive around him, they would be awesome were the scenery not more majestic still. Peter made the sign of the cross. He knew what he had to do. He reached out and touched the prow of the nearest longboat, drawn up on the beach, as if he could heal the ship of what it represented, bring its dead wood back to life. He felt the power of the Spirit. The leader was huge, blond, cuts and scars on his face, lined with the things he had done. Peter reached out and touched the edge of his fur-lined garment.

Then there came a change. The great fierce men no longer held weapons: their ships were burning fiercely, like a pyre. Peter turned and led them towards a cave cut into the hill by the shore. The fire of the dove burning just above his head, he felt it still: he could speak their language; tell them the truth, the necessity of being saved. They followed him inside. They walked some way in the dark, lit only by the living grace of the fire resting on him, then reached a dead end, a wall of earth: but it did not matter, it was meant to be. Peter lay down, and the walls closed around him. The earth came down and filled his mouth.

Colm was shaking him again. The dormitory was shaking, burning. Fire was everywhere. Peter sat up and saw the eyes of a bird looking at him through the fire. With a cry, he reached out his arms to receive it. The beautiful white bird.

Last Breath in Sutherland

The sun bleeds away over the horizon, taking our lives with it. It goes west, leaving shades of red and gold across the heather that fade to black. Two days ago, I was a tenant on the Strath of Kildonan. The factor came, with a piece of paper in one hand and a burning torch in the other. I was used to the dignity of work, to providing for my family. All this is no more. The land is wanted for sheep, for their swirling fat bodies to take the place of generations who have lived and worked this land. I had heard of evictions elsewhere, of the burning of crofts and livelihoods and sometimes of people. There was an old woman burnt out, with her clothes smoking. Her only words were the Gaelic for 'fire', over and over, for the short time she lived afterwards.

Now I am heading to the coast, with my wife and children. I try to keep our heads up during the day, talk cheerfully of food and work where we are going. It is not as if we have any choice. I see the ship waiting at the dock, heading for Canada. We move towards it, touched by the last rays of the sun. It turns a dark, angry red that slants over our heads. This is our last night here. The night our blood flows away.